knit along with

DEBBIE MACOMBER

Summer on Blossom Street

LEISURE ARTS, INC.
Little Rock, Arkansas

EDITORIAL STAFF
Managing Editor: Susan White Sullivan
Knit and Crochet Publications Director: Debra Nettles
Special Projects Director: Susan Frantz Wiles
Senior Prepress Director: Mark Hawkins
Art Publications Director: Rhonda Shelby
Technical Editor: Cathy Hardy
Contributing Editors: Sarah J. Green
    and Lois J. Long
Editorial Writer: Susan McManus Johnson
Art Category Manager: Lora Puls
Graphic Artist: Amy Temple
Production Artist: Janie Wright
Imaging Technicians: Brian Hall, Stephanie Johnson,
    and Mark R. Potter
Photography Manager: Katherine Atchison
Contributing Photographer: Ken West
Contributing Photo Stylist: Mary Tellez
Publishing Systems Administrator: Becky Riddle
Publishing Systems Assistants: Clint Hanson
    and John Rose

BUSINESS STAFF
Vice President and Chief Operations Officer:
    Tom Siebenmorgen
Director of Finance and Administration:
    Laticia Mull Dittrich
Vice President, Sales and Marketing:
    Pam Stebbins
National Accounts Director: Martha Adams
Sales and Services Director: Margaret Reinold
Information Technology Director: Hermine Linz
Controller: Francis Caple
Vice President, Operations: Jim Dittrich
Comptroller, Operations: Rob Thieme
Retail Customer Service Manager: Stan Raynor
Print Production Manager: Fred F. Pruss

ISBN-13: 978-1-60140-912-6
ISBN-10: 1-60140-912-5

10 9 8 7 6 5 4 3 2 1

table of contents

debbie macomber

photo by Nina Subin

Dear Friends,

I confess! I'm among the hundreds of thousands of women (and a few good men) who love to knit, and I have more yarn than one woman has a right to own. I'm crazy about yarn.

Another thing I love about knitting is that it's one of the best ways to de-stress! In *Summer on Blossom Street*, the fifth book of my Blossom Street series, three individuals take a knitting class to help them quit smoking, deal with job stress, and end a bad relationship—all with surprising results!

Whether you're looking for a pleasant distraction or just want to have fun, this companion pattern book has seven delightful **knitting** projects to get you going. And now that another crocheter joined Margaret at the yarn shop, it's only right that we include three exciting **crochet** designs.

If these inspiring patterns have you looking for a way to get your projects organized, you may be interested in the Knit Along with Debbie Macomber Collection. These organizers and accessories include totes, patterns, notions, a CD of printable note cards, and a journal to keep track of projects and supplies. The handy items can be found at *TheLeisureBoutique.com* or your local knitting shop.

The best thing about knitting and crochet is the opportunity they provide for helping others. I've donated the proceeds from sales of my Leisure Arts Knit Along books and the knitter's product line to my favorite charities; including Warm Up America! and World Vision. On page 41, you'll find a block to knit and one to crochet for your own community charity efforts.

I'm so glad these publications and products allow me to be a part of your creative life!

Debbie

meet the characters

Lydia Goetz

Just as I headed down the hallway to turn in for the night, the phone rang.

"Who'd be phoning after ten o'clock?" Brad asked.

I reached for the phone, not knowing what to expect.

"Oh, Lydia, I apologize for contacting you this late." It was Evelyn Boyle, the social worker we'd interviewed with when applying for adoption. It didn't seem possible they would have an infant for us so soon. Nevertheless, my heart raced with excitement.

"Listen, I have a foster child—a girl. It's an emergency and I need a home for Casey for two nights. Casey is attending summer school and unless she finishes the class, she won't go on to the eighth grade. She's only twelve and this is a difficult time for her. Just two nights, Lydia."

"Two nights," I repeated, the hesitation in my voice impossible to disguise. I wanted to help Evelyn, but I was way out of my element when it came to dealing with a troubled young girl.

Phoebe Rylander

Phoebe had just stepped out of A Good Yarn when her cell phone chirped again. She didn't need to check Caller ID to know it was Clark Snowden, her ex-fiancé. Breaking off their engagement shouldn't be this complicated except that Clark made it that way. When she thought about what he'd done, she had to be strong; she couldn't allow him to dissuade her. Not again. This time it was final.

Because she couldn't resist, she checked her cell phone. Clark had left three messages. Determined not to be swayed, she erased them without listening. She dared not hear his voice because she was susceptible. That was one of the reasons she'd impulsively signed up for the knitting class—Knit to Quit. The sign in the yarn shop window seemed to leap out at her like a flashing neon light. If she was going to convince Clark that she was serious, then she was going to need a distraction to help her through the next few weeks.

Bryan "Hutch" Hutchinson

Hutch sat in Dr. Wellington's office. The fact that his physician and former classmate wanted to speak to him privately couldn't be a good sign. Hutch and Dave had been friends for years. Before Hutch took over as CEO of his family's candy business, they'd golfed together every Wednesday afternoon. Golf, like so much else, had been part of the sacrifice he'd needed to make following his father's sudden death.

Dave sat in the high-back leather chair and leaned toward him. "Your blood pressure is far too high. You're working too hard, not exercising enough and your diet is atrocious. You have all the classic symptoms of a man headed for a heart attack. I'll write you a prescription, but what you really need is a change in your lifestyle."

Hutch resisted the urge to groan out loud. "Like what?"

"Diet, start working out, and it wouldn't hurt to take up knitting."

Knitting? Him? "Like I have time for...crafts?"

"It works, Hutch. Give it a try." Dave reached for his pad and wrote out the prescription.

Alix Turner

Friday afternoon, Alix Turner hung up her apron in the kitchen of the French Café. She was finished for the day. Jordan, her husband and a young pastor, wouldn't be done at the church until close to six.

Standing in the alley behind the café, Alix lit her cigarette and took a long drag. She was down to five smokes a day now. Jordan didn't want her smoking. He worried what cigarettes did to her lungs. She fretted about it too; it went without saying that it wouldn't look good for the minister's wife to be seen smoking. Jordan never chastised her, but he wanted her to quit, especially now that they were considering starting a family.

While Alix wanted a baby, the idea overwhelmed her. She had concerns. Doubts. It wasn't like she had grown up with a good example of what a mother should be.

As she stepped across the street, Alix noticed the sign in the window for the new knitting class. Knit to Quit.

cable sampler
scarf

Learn different cable combinations while knitting a scarf for someone special. This project is like getting 7 different designs in one—any of the pattern stitches would make a lovely scarf all by itself.

■■□□ **EASY +**

Lydia's Tip: The Cable patterns are made up of knit and purl stitches and are formed by moving stitches to the front or back of the work allowing the stitches to switch places. Increases are used to allow for the difference in gauge of the Cable Patterns, and then decreases are used to return to the original number of stitches to work the Garter Stitch band that's between each Cable Pattern.

Finished Size: 8" x 57" (20.5 cm x 145 cm)

MATERIALS
Wool Light Weight Yarn **3** LIGHT
[1.75 ounces, 136 yards
(50 grams, 125 meters) per hank]:
  5 hanks
Straight knitting needles, size 6 (4 mm)
  or size needed for gauge
Cable needle

Lydia's Tip: In order for the Scarf to block out as shown, it should be knit with a wool yarn. Synthetics have a tendency to creep back.

GAUGE: In Garter Stitch, 21 sts = 4" (10 cm)

STITCH GUIDE
CABLE 6 BACK (uses 6 sts)
  (abbreviated C6B)
Slip next 3 sts onto cable needle and hold in **back** of work, K3 from left needle, K3 from cable needle.
CABLE 6 FRONT (uses 6 sts)
  (abbreviated C6F)
Slip next 3 sts onto cable needle and hold in **front** of work, K3 from left needle, K3 from cable needle.
CABLE 4 BACK (uses 4 sts)
  (abbreviated C4B)
Slip next 2 sts onto cable needle and hold in **back** of work, K2 from left needle, K2 from cable needle.
CABLE 4 FRONT (uses 4 sts)
  (abbreviated C4F)
Slip next 2 sts onto cable needle and hold in **front** of work, K2 from left needle, K2 from cable needle.

SCARF
Cast on 43 sts loosely.

Lydia's Tip: When instructed to slip a stitch always slip as if to **purl**, with yarn held in front of work. This forms a chain selvedge for the edge of your scarf.

Bottom Band - Rows 1-10: Slip 1, knit across.

Instructions continued on page 8.

"I was thinking of having everyone work on a sampler scarf with a variety of short patterns," Lydia explained. "The scarf shouldn't be too difficult for a beginner and a bit of a challenge to experienced knitters. I think it's going to be a lot of fun."

—*Summer on Blossom Street*

CABLE PATTERN 1

Row 1: Slip 1, K7, P3, (K3, P3) 4 times, K8.

Lydia's Tip: When instructed to increase, work the invisible increase *(Fig. 9, page 45)*, in which you knit the stitch **below** the next stitch and then knit the next stitch.

Row 2 (Right side)**:** Slip 1, K4, P3, (increase 3 times, P3) 5 times, K5: 58 sts.

Row 3: Slip 1, K7, P6, (K3, P6) 4 times, K8.

Row 4: Slip 1, K4, P3, (K6, P3) 5 times, K5.

Row 5: Slip 1, K7, P6, (K3, P6) 4 times, K8.

Row 6: Slip 1, K4, P3, (C6B, P3) 5 times, K5.

Row 7: Slip 1, K7, P6, (K3, P6) 4 times, K8.

Rows 8-13: Repeat Rows 4 and 5, 3 times.

Rows 14-55: Repeat Rows 6-13, 5 times; then repeat Rows 6 and 7 once **more**.

Row 56: Slip 1, K7, K2 tog 3 times *(Fig. 10, page 45)*, (K3, K2 tog 3 times) 4 times, K8: 43 sts.

Band - Next 10 Rows: Slip 1, knit across.

CABLE PATTERN 2

Row 1: Slip 1, K4, purl across to last 5 sts, K5.

Row 2: Slip 1, K4, P6, (K1, increase, K1, P6) 3 times, K5: 46 sts.

Row 3: Slip 1, K 10, P4, (K6, P4) twice, K 11.

Row 4: Slip 1, (K4, P6) 4 times, K5.

Row 5: Slip 1, K 10, P4, (K6, P4) twice, K 11.

Row 6: Slip 1, K4, P6, (C4F, P6) 3 times, K5.

Row 7: Slip 1, K 10, P4, (K6, P4) twice, K 11.

Row 8: Slip 1, (K4, P6) 4 times, K5.

Row 9: Slip 1, K 10, P4, (K6, P4) twice, K 11.

Row 10: Slip 1, K4, P1, K4, (P6, K4) 3 times, P1, K5.

Row 11: Slip 1, K5, P4, (K6, P4) 3 times, K6.

Rows 12 and 13: Repeat Rows 10 and 11.

Row 14: Slip 1, K4, P1, C4F, (P6, C4F) 3 times, P1, K5.

Row 15: Slip 1, K5, P4, (K6, P4) 3 times, K6.

Row 16: Slip 1, K4, P1, K4, (P6, K4) 3 times, P1, K5.

Row 17: Slip 1, K5, P4, (K6, P4) 3 times, K6.

Row 18: Slip 1, (K4, P6) 4 times, K5.

Rows 19-57: Repeat Rows 3-18 twice, then repeat Rows 3-9 once **more**.

Row 58: Slip 1, K 11, K2 tog, (K8, K2 tog) twice, K 12: 43 sts.

Band - Next 10 Rows: Slip 1, knit across.

CABLE PATTERN 3

Row 1: Slip 1, K7, P3, (K3, P3) 4 times, K8.

Row 2: Slip 1, K4, P3, (increase 3 times, P3) 5 times, K5: 58 sts.

Row 3: Slip 1, K7, P6, (K3, P6) 4 times, K8.

Row 4: Slip 1, K4, P3, (K6, P3) 5 times, K5.

Row 5: Slip 1, K7, P6, (K3, P6) 4 times, K8.

Row 6: Slip 1, K4, P3, (C6B, P3) 5 times, K5.

Row 7: Slip 1, K7, P6, (K3, P6) 4 times, K8.

Rows 8-13: Repeat Rows 4 and 5, 3 times.

Row 14: Slip 1, K4, P3, (C6F, P3) 5 times, K5.

Row 15: Slip 1, K7, P6, (K3, P6) 4 times, K8.

Rows 16-21: Repeat Rows 4 and 5, 3 times.

Rows 22-55: Repeat Rows 6-21 twice, then repeat Rows 6 and 7 once **more**.

Row 56: Slip 1, K7, K2 tog 3 times, (K3, K2 tog 3 times) 4 times, K8: 43 sts.

Band - Next 10 Rows: Slip 1, knit across.

CABLE PATTERN 1

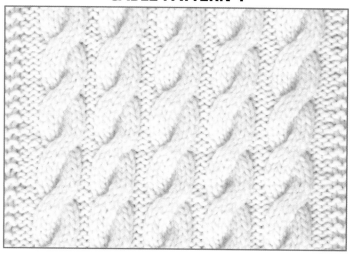

CABLE PATTERN 2

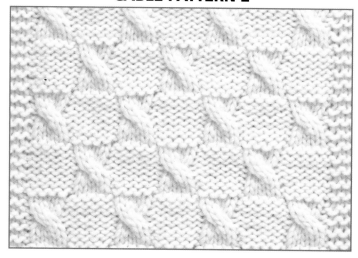

CABLE PATTERN 3

Instructions continued on page 10.

CABLE PATTERN 4

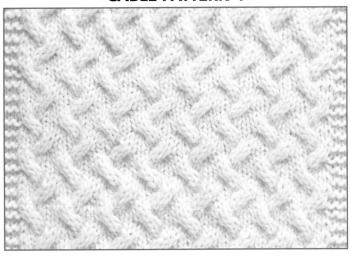

CABLE PATTERN 5

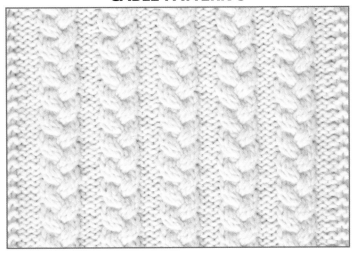

CABLE PATTERN 4
Row 1: Purl across.

Row 2: Slip 1, K5, increase, K3, increase twice, (K2, increase twice) 6 times, K7: 58 sts.

Row 3 AND ALL WRONG SIDE ROWS: Slip 1, K4, purl across to last 5 sts, K5.

Row 4: Slip 1, K4, C4F, (K2, C4F) 7 times, K7.

Row 6: Slip 1, knit across.

Row 8: Slip 1, K6, C4B, (K2, C4B) 7 times, K5.

Row 10: Slip 1, knit across.

Rows 11-57: Repeat Rows 3-10, 5 times; then repeat Rows 3-9 once **more**.

Row 58: Slip 1, K5, K2 tog, K4, K2 tog twice, (K2, K2 tog twice) 6 times, K6: 43 sts.

Band - Next 10 Rows: Slip 1, knit across.

CABLE PATTERN 5
Row 1: Slip 1, K7, P3, (K3, P3) 4 times, K8.

Row 2: Slip 1, K4, P3, (increase 3 times, P3) 5 times, K5: 58 sts.

Row 3 AND ALL WRONG SIDE ROWS: Slip 1, K7, P6, (K3, P6) 4 times, K8.

Row 4: Slip 1, K4, P3, (C4B, K2, P3) 5 times, K5.

Row 6: Slip 1, K4, P3, (K2, C4F, P3) 5 times, K5.

Rows 7-55: Repeat Rows 3-6, 12 times; then repeat Row 3 once **more**.

Row 56: Slip 1, K7, K2 tog 3 times, (K3, K2 tog 3 times) 4 times, K8: 43 sts.

Band - Next 10 Rows: Slip 1, knit across.

CABLE PATTERN 6
Row 1: Slip 1, K4, purl across to last 5 sts, K5.

Row 2: Slip 1, K8, increase, K5, increase twice, (K4, increase twice) 3 times, K8: 52 sts.

Row 3 AND ALL WRONG SIDE ROWS: Slip 1, K4, purl across to last 5 sts, K5.

Row 4: Slip 1, K7, C4B, (K4, C4B) 4 times, K8.

Row 6: Slip 1, K5, C4B, C4F, (K8, C4B, C4F) twice, K6.

Row 8: Slip 1, knit across.

Row 10: Slip 1, K5, C4F, C4B, (K8, C4F, C4B) twice, K6.

Row 12: Slip 1, K7, C4B, (K4, C4B) 4 times, K8.

Row 14: Slip 1, K 13, C4B, C4F, K8, C4B, C4F, K 14.

Row 16: Slip 1, knit across.

Row 18: Slip 1, K 13, C4F, C4B, K8, C4F, C4B, K 14.

Rows 19-59: Repeat Rows 3-18 twice, then repeat Rows 3-11 once **more**.

Row 60: Slip 1, K6, K2 tog twice, ★ K5, K2 tog, K5, K2 tog twice; repeat from ★ once **more**, K9: 44 sts.

Band - Next 10 Rows: Slip 1, knit across.

CABLE PATTERN 7

Row 1: Slip 1, K7, P4, (K3, P2, K3, P4) twice, K8.

Row 2: Slip 1, K4, P3, increase 4 times, P3, ★ increase twice, P3, increase 4 times, P3; repeat from ★ once **more**, K5: 60 sts.

Row 3 AND ALL WRONG SIDE ROWS: Slip 1, K7, P8, (K3, P4, K3, P8) twice, K8.

Row 4: Slip 1, K4, P3, C4F, C4B, (P3, C4F) twice, (C4B, P3) twice, C4F, C4B, P3, K5.

Row 6: Slip 1, (K4, P3, K8, P3) 3 times, K5.

Row 8: Slip 1, K4, P3, C4B, (C4F, P3) twice, C4B, C4F, (P3, C4B) twice, C4F, P3, K5.

Row 10: Slip 1, (K4, P3, K8, P3) 3 times, K5.

Row 12: Slip 1, K4, P3, C4B, (C4F, P3) twice, C4B, C4F, (P3, C4B) twice, C4F, P3, K5.

Row 14: Slip 1, (K4, P3, K8, P3) 3 times, K5.

CABLE PATTERN 6

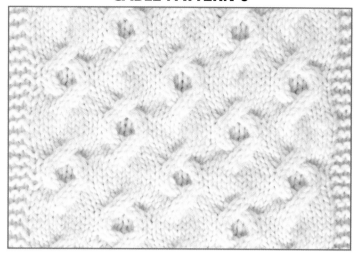

CABLE PATTERN 7

Row 16: Slip 1, K4, P3, C4F, C4B, (P3, C4F) twice, (C4B, P3) twice, C4F, C4B, P3, K5.

Row 18: Slip 1, (K4, P3, K8, P3) 3 times, K5.

Rows 19-57: Repeat Rows 3-18 twice, then repeat Rows 3-9 once **more**.

Row 58: Slip 1, K4, K2 tog, K1, K2 tog 4 times, ★ K3, K2 tog twice, K3, K2 tog 4 times; repeat from ★ once **more**, K8: 43 sts.

Top Band - Last 10 Rows: Slip 1, knit across.

Bind off all sts loosely in **knit**.

Design by Bev Galeskas
Fiber Trends Inc.
www.fibertrends.com

11

baby blanket

A pleasant distraction, indeed—knitting this sweet blanket in DK weight yarn is sure to focus your thoughts on such pleasant matters as the sound of a baby's laughter.

◖■◻▭ **EASY**

Finished Size: 32" x 40¹⁄₂" (81.5 cm x 103 cm)

MATERIALS

Light Weight Yarn
[4.25 ounces, 333 yards
(120 grams, 304 meters) per skein]:
  3 skeins
29" (73.5 cm) Circular knitting needle,
  size 6 (4 mm) **or** size needed for gauge
Optional for girl: ¹⁄₄" (7 mm) wide Ribbon -
  5¹⁄₂ yards (5 meters)

GAUGE: In pattern, one repeat (11 sts) and
16 rows = 2¹⁄₄" (5.75 cm)

Gauge Swatch: 4¹⁄₂" x 4" (11.5 cm x 10 cm)
Cast on 22 sts.
Row 1: Purl across.
Row 2: Knit across.
Row 3: P4, K1, P2, K9, P2, K1, P3.
Row 4: K3, Front Cross, Back Cross, K7,
Front Cross, Back Cross, K4.
Rows 5-28: Repeat Rows 1-4, 6 times.
Bind off all sts in **purl**.

STITCH GUIDE

FRONT CROSS

Knit second st on left needle *(Fig. 1a)* making sure **not** to drop off, then knit the first st *(Fig. 1b)* letting both sts drop off the needle.

Fig. 1a

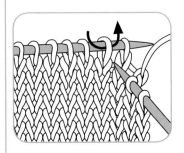

Fig. 1b

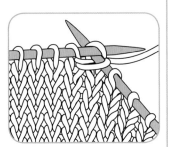

BACK CROSS

Working **behind** first st on left needle, knit into the back of second st *(Fig. 2a)* making sure not to drop off, then knit the first st *(Fig. 2b)* letting both sts drop off the needle.

Fig. 2a

Fig. 2b

Lydia's Tip: A Cross forms a 2 stitch cable, without using a cable needle. Isn't it a great technique?

Instructions continued on page 14.

The thought of having Jordan's baby excited Alix, if only she could give up these stupid smokes. She decided she'd knit a baby blanket. If she started a special blanket for their yet-to-be conceived child, that would show Jordan she was serious about quitting.

Alix's eyes were drawn toward the DK weight yarn in soft pastel colors. Lydia had them displayed in the bins closest to the cash register.

—*Summer on Blossom Street*

BODY

Cast on 157 sts.

Rows 1-6: Knit across.

Row 7 (Right side - Eyelet row)**:** K4, YO *(Fig. 7a, page 44)*, K2 tog *(Fig. 10, page 45)*, (YO, K2 tog) across to last 3 sts, K3.

Row 8: K4, purl across to last 4 sts, K4.

Row 9: Knit across.

Row 10: K4, purl across to last 4 sts, K4.

Row 11: K4, YO, K2 tog, knit across to last 5 sts, YO, K2 tog, K3.

Row 12: K4, P1, K1, P2, (K9, P2) across to last 6 sts, K1, P1, K4.

Row 13: K5, Front Cross, Back Cross, ★ K7, Front Cross, Back Cross; repeat from ★ across to last 5 sts, K5.

Repeat Rows 10-13 for pattern until Body measures approximately 39¹/₂" (100.5 cm) from cast on edge, ending by working Row 11.

Next Row: K4, purl across to last 4 sts, K4.

Next Row (Eyelet row)**:** K4, (YO, K2 tog) across to last 3 sts, K3.

Last 6 Rows: Knit across.

Bind off all sts in **knit**.

Lydia's Tip: To make this blanket a little fancy for a girl, weave ribbon through eyelets on each side and tie a bow in each corner.

washcloth
to crochet

A great beginner project, and one that can be crocheted without constantly looking at the instructions, this washcloth makes an ideal gift for wedding showers and house warming parties. It's also perfect for introducing a pre-teen to yarn crafts, as Lydia discovered.

I returned to the table where I'd left Casey. To my amazement, Margaret was sitting with her. Together, the two of them were crocheting.

"She's crocheting a washcloth," righteousness rang in my sister Margaret's tone. "Look at her work, Lydia, the girl's a natural."

—Lydia

Summer on Blossom Street

 ◼◻◻◻ **BEGINNER**

MATERIALS

100% Cotton Medium Weight Yarn **4 MEDIUM**
[1.5 ounces, 68 yards
(42 grams, 62 meters) per skein]:
  1 skein makes one washcloth
Crochet hook, size H (5 mm)

Lydia's Tip: Gauge doesn't matter very much. If your Washcloth measures approximately 8" (20.5 cm) wide, you can make a square cloth from one skein of yarn.

BODY
Ch 36.

Row 1: Sc in second ch from hook and in each ch across: 35 sc.

Row 2: Ch 1, turn; sc in both loops of first sc, sc in Back Loop Only of next sc *(Fig. 20, page 47)*, ★ sc in Front Loop Only of next sc, sc in Back Loop Only of next sc; repeat from ★ across to last sc, sc in **both** loops of last sc.

Repeat Row 2 for pattern until Washcloth measures approximately 8" (20.5 cm) from beginning ch; finish off.

Weave in all yarn ends.

memories of paris scarf

For a luxurious yarn, you need an elegant knitting pattern. This lacy scarf has both, proving how doubly rewarding knitting can be.

●●□□ **EASY**

Finished Size: 8" x 55" (20.5 cm x 139.5 cm)

MATERIALS
 Light Weight Yarn 🔵**3**
 [.75 ounces, 116 yards
 (25 grams, 106 meters) per ball]:
  3 balls
 Straight knitting needles, size 6 (4 mm)
  or size needed for gauge

GAUGE: In pattern,
     2 repeats (12 sts) = 3" (7.5 cm)

BODY
Cast on 33 sts.

Rows 1-3: K1, (P1, K1) across.

Lydia's Tip: If you haven't knit many lace patterns, this is a good place to start. It's a good idea to check to make sure you made all of the yarn overs after every right side row.

Row 4 (Right side)**:** K1, (P1, K1) twice, K2 tog *(Fig. 10, page 45)*, YO *(Fig. 7a, page 44)*, K1, YO, K2 tog tbl *(Fig. 11, page 45)*, K1, ★ K2 tog, YO, K1, YO, K2 tog tbl, K1; repeat from ★ across to last 4 sts, (P1, K1) twice.

Row 5: K1, P1, K1, purl across to last 3 sts, K1, P1, K1.

Row 6: (K1, P1) twice, K2 tog, YO, K3, ★ YO, [slip 2 sts separately as if to **knit**, K1, P2SSO *(Fig. 13, page 46)*], YO, K3; repeat from ★ across to last 6 sts, YO, K2 tog tbl, (P1, K1) twice.

Row 7: K1, P1, K1, purl across to last 3 sts, K1, P1, K1.

Row 8: K1, (P1, K1) twice ★ YO, K2 tog tbl, K1, K2 tog, YO, K1; repeat from ★ across to last 4 sts, (P1, K1) twice.

Row 9: K1, P1, K1, purl across to last 3 sts, K1, P1, K1.

Row 10: (K1, P1) twice, K2, YO, slip 2 sts separately as if to **knit**, K1, P2SSO, ★ YO, K3, YO, slip 2 sts separately as if to **knit**, K1, P2SSO; repeat from ★ across to last 6 sts, YO, K2, (P1, K1) twice.

Row 11: K1, P1, K1, purl across to last 3 sts, K1, P1, K1.

Repeat Rows 4-11 for pattern until Body measures approximately 54½" (138.5 cm) from cast on edge, ending by working Row 10.

Last 3 Rows: K1, (P1, K1) across.

Bind off all sts in pattern.

Nine-year-old Ellen Roche had slept most of the transatlantic flight from Paris, but not Anne Marie. Instead, she'd wrapped her arm around her young daughter and sifted through each and every precious memory of their two week vacation. The youngster had picked up French phrases with surprising ease. Anne Marie had picked up some wonderful yarn while in Paris and was keen about knitting it up. A scarf would be perfect.

—*Summer on Blossom Street*

poncho

Easy stitches and easy construction make this design popular with new knitters. It's fun to see the lacy checkerboard pattern appear under your fingers!

◼◼◻◻ **EASY**

Size	Misses Size
X-Small/Small	4-8
Medium/Large	10-16
X-Large	18-20

Size Note: Instructions are written for size X-Small/Small with sizes Medium/Large and X-Large in braces { }. Instructions will be easier to read if you circle all the numbers pertaining to your size. If only one number is given, it applies to all sizes.

MATERIALS

Medium Weight Yarn **MEDIUM (4)**
[3 ounces, 185 yards
(85 grams, 170 meters) per skein]:
   4{5-7} skeins
Straight knitting needles, size 7 (4.5 mm)
   or size needed for gauge
Yarn needle

GAUGE: In pattern, one repeat (12 sts)
   and 24 rows = 3" (7.5 cm)

Gauge Swatch: 7" x 3" (17.75 cm x 7.5 cm)
Cast on 28 sts.
Rows 1-24: Work same as Panel, Rows 4-27.
Bind off all sts in **knit**.

Lydia's Tip: The Seed Stitch border at the bottom and side edges trim the Poncho nicely. The top edge of each Panel will be sewn to the side of the opposite Panel and won't need a border.

PANEL (Make 2)
Cast on 64{76-88} sts.

Row 1: (K1, P1) across.

Row 2 (Right side): (P1, K1) across.

Note: Loop a short piece of yarn around any stitch to mark Row 2 as **right** side.

Row 3: (K1, P1) across.

Row 4: (P1, K1) 4 times, (YO, K2 tog) 3 times (*Fig. 7a, page 44 and Fig. 10, page 45)*, ★ (P1, K1) 3 times, (YO, K2 tog) 3 times; repeat from ★ across to last 2 sts, P1, K1.

Row 5: K1, P7, ★ K1, (P1, K1) twice, P7; repeat from ★ across to last 8 sts, (K1, P1) across.

Row 6: (P1, K1) 4 times, (K2 tog, YO) 3 times (*Fig. 7b, page 44)*, ★ (P1, K1) 3 times, (K2 tog, YO) 3 times; repeat from ★ across to last 2 sts, P1, K1.

Row 7: K1, P7, ★ K1, (P1, K1) twice, P7; repeat from ★ across to last 8 sts, (K1, P1) across.

Rows 8-15: Repeat Rows 4-7 twice.

Row 16: P1, K1, (YO, K2 tog) 3 times, ★ (P1, K1) 3 times, (YO, K2 tog) 3 times; repeat from ★ across to last 8 sts, (P1, K1) across.

Row 17: K1, (P1, K1) 3 times, P7, ★ K1, (P1, K1) twice, P7; repeat from ★ across to last 2 sts, K1, P1.

Instructions continued on page 39.

I'd found a pattern for a poncho that several teen girls had knitted, and I was sure Casey would like one. I would have loved to teach her to knit, but she'd rejected that notion on more than one occasion.

—Lydia
Summer on Blossom Street

cody's pullover

This drop-shoulder sweater gives an active child like Lydia's son Cody plenty of room to move around. The pattern works equally well for girls, although you may decide to change your yarn colors.

⬛⬛☐☐ **EASY**

Size	Finished Chest Measurement	
4	27"	(68.5 cm)
6	28¹/₂"	(72.5 cm)
8	30"	(76 cm)
10	31¹/₂"	(80 cm)
12	33"	(84 cm)
14	34¹/₂"	(87.5 cm)

Size Note: Instructions are written with sizes 4, 6, and 8 in the first set of braces { } and sizes 10, 12, and 14 in the second set of braces. Instructions will be easier to read if you circle all the numbers pertaining to your size. If only one number is given, it applies to all sizes.

MATERIALS
Medium Weight Yarn **(4)** MEDIUM
[3.5 ounces, 170 yards
(100 grams, 156 meters) per skein]:
   Brown - {2-2-3}{3-3-4} skeins
   Green - {2-2-2}{3-3-3} skeins
Straight knitting needles, sizes 6 (4 mm)
  and 7 (4.5 mm) **or** sizes needed for gauge
16" (40.5 cm) Circular knitting needle,
  size 6 (4 mm)
Stitch holder
Markers
Yarn needle

GAUGE: With larger size needles,
     in pattern,
     18 sts and 34 rows = 4¹/₂" (11.5 cm)

Gauge Swatch: 4¹/₂" (11.5 cm) square
With larger size needles and Brown,
cast on 18 sts.
Row 1: (K3, P3) across.
Row 2: (P3, K3) across.
Rows 3-34: Repeat Rows 1 and 2, 16 times, changing colors every 2 rows.
Bind off all sts in **knit**.

Lydia's Tip: The pattern is essentially Garter Stitch, but by alternating 3 knit and 3 purl stitches, the color pattern is formed – even though only one color is worked at a time. Once you work the first row, all you have to remember is to work each edge stitch in Stockinette stitch, and then to knit the purl stitches and purl the knit stitches as they face you.

BACK
RIBBING
With smaller size needles and Brown, cast on {56-58-62}{64-68-70} sts.

Work in K1, P1 ribbing for 1" (2.5 cm), increasing {0-1-0}{1-0-1} st(s) on last row *(Figs. 8a & b, page 44 and Zeros, page 43)*: {56-59-62}{65-68-71} sts.

BODY
Change to larger size needles.

Drop Brown; carry unused yarn along edge of piece.

Row 1 (Right side)**:** With Green, K4, P3, (K3, P3) across to last {1-4-1}{4-1-4} st(s), K {1-4-1}{4-1-4}.

Instructions continued on page 22.

I took a seat and pulled out my knitting. I knew I'd have a full hour to work on a sweater I was knitting for Cody. He'd chosen the colors himself, which were a dark green and brown that looked almost camouflage when knit together.

—Lydia
Summer on Blossom Street

Note: Loop a short piece of yarn around any stitch to mark Row 1 as **right** side.

Row 2: P {4-1-4}{1-4-1}, K3, (P3, K3) across to last st, P1.

Working 2 rows with each color, repeat Rows 1 and 2 for pattern until Back measures approximately {15½-17-18½}{20-22-24½}"/{39.5-43-47}{51-56-62} cm from cast on edge, ending by working just one row with either color.

Bind off all sts in pattern.

FRONT

Work same as Back until Front measures approximately {2-2-2}{2½-2½-2½}"/{5-5-5}{6.5-6.5-6.5} cm less than Back, ending by working one row with Brown.

NECK SHAPING

Both sides of Neck are worked at the same time, using separate yarn for **each** side. Maintain established pattern throughout.

Row 1: Work across {25-26-27}{28-29-29} sts, slip next {6-7-8}{9-10-13} sts onto st holder; with second yarn, work across: {25-26-27}{28-29-29} sts **each** side.

Rows 2-4 (Decrease rows): Work across to within 2 sts of Neck edge, decrease *(see Decreases, pages 45 and 46)*; with second yarn, decrease, work across: {22-23-24}{25-26-26} sts **each** side.

Continue to decrease one stitch at **each** Neck edge, every other row, 3 times: {19-20-21}{22-23-23} sts **each** side.

Work even until Front measures same as Back, ending by working just one row with either color.

Bind off all sts in pattern.

Sew shoulder seams.

Place a marker on **each** side of Front and Back {6¼-6½-7¼}{7¾-8-8½}"/{16-16.5-18.5}{19.5-20.5-21.5} cm down from shoulder seam.

SLEEVE
BODY

With **right** side facing, using larger size needles and Brown, pick up {50-53-59}{62-65-68} sts evenly spaced between markers *(Fig. 16a, page 46)*.

Row 1: P {4-1-1}{4-1-4}, K3, (P3, K3) across to last st, P1.

Row 2: With Green, K4, P3, (K3, P3) across to last {1-4-4}{1-4-1} st(s), K {1-4-4}{1-4-1}.

Row 3: P {4-1-1}{4-1-4}, K3, (P3, K3) across to last st, P1.

Working 2 rows with each color, repeat Rows 2 and 3 for pattern until Sleeve measures approximately 2" (5 cm).

Next Row (Decrease row): Decrease, work across to last 2 sts, decrease: {48-51-57}{60-63-66} sts.

Work in established pattern, decreasing one stitch at **each** edge, then every sixth row, {0-1-2}{3-9-10} times; then decrease every fourth row, {11-11-12}{13-7-8} times: {26-27-29}{28-31-30} sts.

Work even until Sleeve measures approximately {8¼-9¼-10½}{12-13½-15}"/{21-23.5-26.5} {30.5-34.5-38} cm, ending by working two rows with Green.

RIBBING
Change to smaller size needles.

With Brown and decreasing {0-1-1}{0-1-0} st(s) at end of first row, work in K1, P1 ribbing for 2" (5 cm): {26-26-28}{28-30-30} sts.

Bind off all sts in ribbing.

Repeat for second Sleeve.

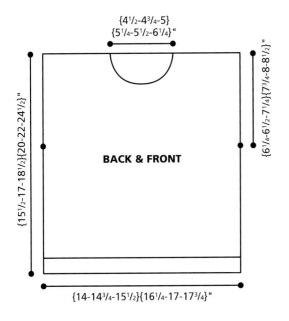

{4½-4¾-5}
{5¼-5½-6¼}"

{15½-17-18½}{20-22-24½}"

BACK & FRONT

{6¼-6½-7¼}{7¾-8-8½}"

{14-14¾-15½}{16¼-17-17¾}"

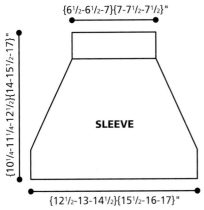

{6½-6½-7}{7-7½-7½}"

{10¼-11¼-12½}{14-15½-17}"

SLEEVE

{12½-13-14½}{15½-16-17}"

Note: Pullover includes two edge stitches.

FINISHING
NECK RIBBING
With **right** side facing, using circular needle and Brown, pick up {12-12-12}{14-14-14} sts evenly spaced along left Front Neck edge, knit {6-7-8}{9-10-13} sts from st holder, pick up {12-12-12}{14-14-14} sts evenly spaced along right Front Neck edge, pick up {18-19-20}{21-22-25} sts evenly spaced across Back neck edge *(Fig. 16b, page 46)*; place marker to mark beginning of round *(see Markers, page 43)*: {48-50-52}{58-60-66} sts.

Work in K1, P1 ribbing for 1" (2.5 cm).

Bind off all sts **loosely** in ribbing.

Weave underarm and side in one continuous seam *(Fig. 17, page 47)*.

reese's vest

Years ago, Jacqueline was one of Lydia's first knitting students, and she quickly became one of her best customers. It never surprises Lydia anymore to see her friend buy the most expensive yarn in her shop. If Lydia mentioned that the vest would also look quite handsome in a less costly yarn, Jacqueline would simply be amused.

■■■□ INTERMEDIATE

Size	Finished Chest Measurement	
34	36"	(91.5 cm)
36	38"	(96.5 cm)
38	40"	(101.5 cm)
40	42¹/₂"	(108 cm)
42	44"	(112 cm)
44	46"	(117 cm)

Size Note: Instructions are written with sizes 34, 36, and 38 in the first set of braces { } and sizes 40, 42, and 44 in the second set of braces. Instructions will be easier to read if you circle all the numbers pertaining to your size. If only one number is given, it applies to all sizes.

MATERIALS
Fine Weight Yarn ● **2** FINE
[1.75 ounces, 110 yards (50 grams, 101 meters) per skein]:
   {6-7-7}{7-8-8} skeins
Straight knitting needles, sizes 2 (2.75 mm) and 3 (3.25 mm) **or** sizes needed for gauge
16" (40.5 cm) Circular knitting needle, size 2 (2.75 mm)
Cable needle
Markers
Tapestry needle

GAUGE: With larger size needle, in Reverse Stockinette Stitch, 23 sts and 30 rows = 4" (10 cm)

STITCH GUIDE

TWIST 2 LEFT
Slip next st onto cable needle and hold in **front** of work, P1 from left needle, K1 tbl from cable needle **(Fig. 6, page 44)**.

TWIST 2 RIGHT
Slip next st onto cable needle and hold in **back** of work, K1 tbl from left needle, P1 from cable needle.

TWIST 2
Slip next st onto cable needle and hold in **back** of work, P1 tbl from left needle, P1 tbl from cable neede.

FRONT
RIBBING
With smaller size needles, cast on {106-112-118} {124-128-134} sts.

Work in K1, P1 ribbing for 14 rows.

Next Row (Increase row)**:** Work across {39-42-45}{48-50-53} sts in established ribbing, place marker **(see Markers, page 43)**, knit into the front **and** into the back of the next st **(Figs. 8a & b, page 44)**, (work across 8 sts, knit into the front **and** into the back of the next st) 3 times, place marker, work across last {39-42-45}{48-50-53} sts: {110-116-122}{128-132-138} sts.

BODY
Change to larger size needles.

Row 1 (Right side)**:** Purl across to marker, ★ twist 2 left twice, P2, twist 2 right, twist 2 left, P2, twist 2 right twice; repeat from ★ once **more**, purl across.

Instructions continued on page 26.

The bell above the door chimed. It was Jacqueline Donovan, a good friend of mine. Jacqueline and Reese, her husband, had recently taken a cruise to Hawaii and were only just back. As she headed toward the yarn bins, Jacqueline was filled with stories. She'd read a knitting magazine on the airplane and simply had to knit this wonderfully intricate vest for Reese. She chose a lovely alpaca in a deep brown shade and I rang up the purchase.

—Lydia
*Summer on
Blossom Street*

25

Row 2: Knit across to marker, (K1, P1 tbl) twice, (K2, P1 tbl) 3 times, (K1, P1 tbl, K2, P1 tbl) twice, (K2, P1 tbl) twice, K1, P1 tbl, knit across.

Row 3: Purl across to marker, P1, † twist 2 left twice, twist 2 right, P2, twist 2 left, twist 2 right twice †, P2, repeat from † to † once, purl across.

Row 4: Knit across to marker, K2, † P1 tbl, K1, P2 tbl, K4, P2 tbl, K1, P1 tbl †, K4, repeat from † to † once, knit across.

Row 5: Purl across to marker, P2, twist 2 left twice, P4, twist 2 right twice, P4, twist 2 left twice, P4, twist 2 right twice, purl across.

Row 6: Knit across to marker, K3, P1 tbl, K1, P1 tbl, K4, P1 tbl, K1, P2 tbl, K4, P2 tbl, K1, P1 tbl, K4, P1 tbl, K1, P1 tbl, knit across.

Row 7: Purl across to marker, P3, twist 2 left twice, P2, twist 2 right twice, twist 2 left, P2, twist 2 right, twist 2 left twice, P2, twist 2 right twice, purl across.

Row 8: Knit across to marker, K4, (P1 tbl, K1, P1 tbl, K2) twice, P1 tbl, K2, P1 tbl, (K2, P1 tbl, K1, P1 tbl) twice, knit across.

Row 9: Purl across to marker, P4, twist 2 left twice, twist 2 right twice, P2, twist 2 left, twist 2 right, P2, twist 2 left twice, twist 2 right twice, purl across.

Row 10: Knit across to marker, K5, † P1 tbl, K1, twist 2, K1, P1 tbl †, K4, twist 2, K4, repeat from † to † once, knit across.

Row 11: Purl across to marker, P4, twist 2 right twice, twist 2 left twice, P2, twist 2 right, twist 2 left, P2, twist 2 right twice, twice 2 left twice, purl across.

Row 12: Knit across to marker, K4, (P1 tbl, K1, P1 tbl, K2) twice, P1 tbl, K2, P1 tbl, (K2, P1 tbl, K1, P1 tbl) twice, knit across.

Row 13: Purl across to marker, P3, twist 2 right twice, P2, twist 2 left twice, twist 2 right, P2, twist 2 left, twist 2 right twice, P2, twist 2 left twice, purl across.

Row 14: Knit across to marker, K3, P1 tbl, K1, P1 tbl, K4, P1 tbl, K1, P2 tbl, K4, P2 tbl, K1, P1 tbl, K4, P1 tbl, K1, P1 tbl, knit across.

Row 15: Purl across to marker, P2, twist 2 right twice, P4, twist 2 left twice, P4, twist 2 right twice, P4, twist 2 left twice, purl across.

Row 16: Knit across to marker, K2, † P1 tbl, K1, P2 tbl, K4, P2 tbl, K1, P1 tbl †, K4, repeat from † to † once, knit across.

Row 17: Purl across to marker, P1, † twist 2 right twice, twist 2 left, P2, twist 2 right, twist 2 left twice †, P2, repeat from † to † once, purl across.

Row 18: Knit across to marker, (K1, P1 tbl) twice, (K2, P1 tbl) 3 times, (K1, P1 tbl, K2, P1 tbl) twice, (K2, P1 tbl) twice, K1, P1 tbl, knit across.

Row 19: Purl across to marker, ★ twist 2 right twice, P2, twist 2 left, twist 2 right, P2, twist 2 left twice; repeat from ★ once **more**, purl across.

Row 20: Knit across to marker, P1 tbl, K1, P1 tbl, K4, twist 2, K4, P1 tbl, K1, twist 2, K1, P1 tbl, K4, twist 2, K4, P1 tbl, K1, P1 tbl, knit across.

Rows 21 thru {92-90-90}{88-88-86}: Repeat Rows 1-20, 3 times; then repeat Rows 1 thru {12-10-10}{8-8-6} once **more**.

ARMHOLE SHAPING

Maintain established pattern throughout.

Rows 1 and 2: Bind off {7-7-8}{8-9-10} sts, work across: {96-102-106}{112-114-118} sts.

Row 3 (Decrease row)**:** P1, P2 tog *(Fig. 14, page 46)*, work across to last 3 sts, SSP *(Fig. 15, page 46)*, P1: {94-100-104}{110-112-116} sts.

Row 4 (Decrease row)**:** K1, SSK *(Figs. 12a-c, page 45)*, work across to last 3 sts, K2 tog *(Fig. 10, page 45)*, K1: {92-98-102} {108-110-114} sts.

Continue to decrease one stitch at **each** Armhole edge, every row {1-1-2}{2-2-3} time(s) **more**; then decrease every other row, {4-4-4}{5-5-5} times: {82-88-90}{94-96-98} sts.

Work even until a total of six, 20-row repeats (120 rows) have been completed above the ribbing and ending by working pattern Row 20.

NECK SHAPING

Both sides of Neck are worked at the same time using separate yarn for **each** side.

Row 1: Purl across to within 2 sts of marker, SSP, † twist 2 left twice, P2, twist 2 right, twist 2 left, P2, twist 2 right twice †; with second yarn, repeat from † to † once, P2 tog, purl across: {40-43-44}{46-47-48} sts **each** side.

Row 2: Knit across to marker, † (K1, P1 tbl) twice, (K2, P1 tbl) 3 times, K1, P1 tbl, K1 †; with second yarn, repeat from † to † once, knit across.

Row 3: Purl across to within 2 sts of marker, SSP, † P1, twist 2 left twice, twist 2 right, P2, twist 2 left, twist 2 right twice, P1 †; with second yarn, repeat from † to † once, P2 tog, purl across: {39-42-43}{45-46-47} sts **each** side.

Row 4: Knit across to marker, † K2, P1 tbl, K1, P2 tbl, K4, P2 tbl, K1, P1 tbl, K2 †; with second yarn, repeat from † to † once, knit across.

Row 5: Purl across to within 2 sts of marker, SSP, † P2, twist 2 left twice, P4, twist 2 right twice, P2 †; with second yarn, repeat from † to † once, P2 tog, purl across: {38-41-42}{44-45-46} sts **each** side.

Row 6: Knit across to marker, † K3, P1 tbl, K1, P1 tbl, K4, P1 tbl, K1, P1 tbl, K3 †; with second yarn, repeat from † to † once, knit across.

Row 7: Purl across to within 2 sts of marker, SSP, † P3, twist 2 left twice, P2, twist 2 right twice, P3 †; with second yarn, repeat from † to † once, P2 tog, purl across: {37-40-41}{43-44-45} sts **each** side.

Row 8: Knit across to marker, † K4, P1 tbl, K1, P1 tbl, K2, P1 tbl, K1, P1 tbl, K4 †; with second yarn, repeat from † to † once, knit across.

Row 9: Purl across to within 2 sts of marker, SSP, † P4, twist 2 left twice, twist 2 right twice, P4 †; with second yarn, repeat from † to † once, P2 tog, purl across: {36-39-40}{42-43-44} sts **each** side.

Row 10: Knit across to marker, † K5, P1 tbl, K1, twist 2, K1, P1 tbl, K5 †; with second yarn, repeat from † to † once, knit across.

Row 11: Purl across to within 2 sts of marker, SSP, † P4, twist 2 right twice, twist 2 left twice, P4 †; with second yarn, repeat from † to † once, P2 tog, purl across: {35-38-39}{41-42-43} sts **each** side.

Instructions continued on page 28.

lap robe
to crochet

A Granny Square is a classic pattern that can take on all kinds of personality, depending on the yarn color(s) you choose. It's also an excellent way to use up yarn scraps from previous projects. Lydia is a knitter through-and-through, but it makes her happy to see Casey involved with such a creative pursuit as crochet.

● □ □ □ **BEGINNER**

Finished Size: 34" x 47" (86.5 cm x 119.5 cm)

MATERIALS
Medium Weight Yarn
[3.5 ounces, 207 yards
(100 grams, 188 meters) per skein]:
Colors A and B - 8 skeins total
Note: Our model used 4 skeins **each** color
Crochet hook, size G (4 mm) **or** size needed
for gauge
Yarn needle

GAUGE: Each Square = 6½" (16.5 cm)

Gauge Swatch: 3" (7.5 cm) square
Work same as Square through Rnd 3.

SQUARE (Make 35)
Ch 5; join with slip st to form a ring.

Rnd 1 (Right side)**:** Ch 3 **(counts as first dc, now and throughout)**, 2 dc in ring, (ch 1, 3 dc in ring) 3 times, sc in top of first dc to form last corner sp: 12 dc and 4 corner sps.

Note: Loop a short piece of yarn around any stitch to mark Rnd 1 as **right** side.

You can continue with the same color or change colors by dropping the color just used then pulling the new color through as you make the first ch.

Rnd 2: Ch 1, (sc, ch 3) twice in first corner sp and in each corner ch-1 sp around; join with slip st to first sc: 8 sc and 8 ch-3 sps.

Rnd 3: Slip st in next 2 chs, ch 3, 2 dc in same ch-3 sp, ch 1, 3 dc in next ch-3 sp, ch 1, ★ (3 dc, ch 1) twice in next corner ch-3 sp, 3 dc in next ch-3 sp, ch 1; repeat from ★ around, 3 dc in same corner sp as first dc, sc in top of first dc to form last corner sp: 36 dc and 12 sps.

Lydia's Tip: Make as many color combinations as you wish, changing colors after odd numbered rnds as desired.

Rnd 4: Ch 1, (sc, ch 3) twice in first corner sp, ★ (sc in next ch-1 sp, ch 3) across to next corner ch-1 sp, (sc, ch 3) twice in corner ch-1 sp; repeat from ★ 2 times **more**, (sc in next ch-1 sp, ch 3) across; join with slip st to first sc: 16 sc and 16 ch-3 sps.

Rnd 5: Slip st in next 2 chs, ch 3, 2 dc in same ch-3 sp, ch 1, ★ (3 dc in next ch-3 sp, ch 1) across to next corner ch-3 sp, (3 dc, ch 1) twice in corner ch-3 sp; repeat from ★ 2 times **more**, (3 dc in next ch-3 sp, ch 1) across, 3 dc in same corner sp as first dc, sc in top of first dc to form last corner sp: 60 dc and 20 sps.

Rnds 6 and 7: Repeat Rnds 4 and 5: 84 dc and 28 sps.

Finish off leaving a long end for sewing.

Instructions continued on page 39.

Since the afternoon at the shop when she'd learned to crochet, Casey had crocheted five washcloths now and I gave her some leftover yarn for granny squares, which she seemed to enjoy making.

—Lydia
Summer on Blossom Street

socks
for hutch

Phoebe is surprised at how much she's enjoying learning to knit. It now looks as though she'll need a new project to start at the end of the Knit to Quit class—which makes a yarn display at the baseball stadium just a little too tempting.

Size	Finished Foot Circumference
Women	
Small	7¹/₂" (19 cm)
Medium	8" (20.5 cm)
Large	8¹/₂" (21.5 cm)
Men	
Small	9" (23 cm)
Medium	9¹/₂" (24 cm)
Large	10" (25.5 cm)

Size Note: Instructions are written with Women sizes in the first set of braces { } and Men sizes in the second set of braces. Instructions will be easier to read if you circle all the numbers pertaining to your size. If only one number is given, it applies to all sizes.

MATERIALS

Super Fine Weight Self Striping Yarn
[1.75 ounces, 166 yards
(50 grams, 140 meters) per skein]:
   {2-3-3}{3-3-4} skeins
Set of 5 double pointed knitting needles,
   sizes 3 (3.25 mm) **and** 4 (3.5 mm) **or** sizes
   needed for gauge
Stitch holders - 2
Split-ring markers
Tapestry needle

GAUGE: With smaller size needles,
   in Stockinette Stitch,
   28 sts and 36 rnds = 4" (10 cm)

CUFF
With larger size needle, cast on {52-56-60} {64-68-72} sts.

Slip {13-14-15}{16-17-18} sts onto each of 3 double pointed needles, leaving {13-14-15} {16-17-18} sts on the fourth needle *(Fig. 5, page 44)*.

Lydia's Tip: The yarn end indicates the beginning of the round.

Work in K1, P1 ribbing until ribbing measures approximately 1¹/₂" (4 cm) from cast on edge.

LEG
Change to smaller size needles.

Row 1: Knit around.

Row 2: (K1, P1) around.

Repeat Rows 1 and 2 until piece measures approximately {5¹/₂-6-6¹/₂}{7-7¹/₂-8}"/{14-15-16.5} {18-19-20.5} cm from cast on edge **or** 1" (2.5 cm) less than desired length.

Knit each round (Stockinette Stitch) for 1" (2.5 cm).

Instructions continued on page 34.

Phoebe chose sock yarn in the Seattle Mariners home team colors.

"What did you buy?" Hutch asked when she rejoined him in the stands.

"I'm going to learn to knit socks. Do you like the colors," she asked.

"You bet." He smiled down on her and seemed to have a hard time looking away.

"I thought I'd knit them up for you," she whispered, having trouble finding her voice.

—*Summer on Blossom Street*

HEEL FLAP

Dividing Stitches: Knit across first needle; slip sts from the next 2 needles onto 2 separate st holders for Instep to be worked later; **turn**.

Lydia's Tip: The following pattern will make the Heel dense and will help prevent it from wearing out. Work Row 1 across both needles onto one needle. The Heel Flap will be worked back and forth across these {26-28-30}{32-34-36} sts.

When instructed to slip a stitch, always slip as if to **purl** with yarn held to **wrong** side.

Row 1: (Slip 1, P1) across.

Row 2: (Slip 1, K1) across.

Repeat Rows 1 and 2, {12-13-14}{15-16-17} times; then repeat Row 1 once **more**.

TURN HEEL

Begin working in short rows as follows:

Row 1: Slip 1, K {14-16-18}{20-22-24}, SSK *(Figs. 12a-c, page 45)*, K1, leave remaining 8 sts unworked; **turn**.

Row 2: Slip 1, P {5-7-9}{11-13-15}, P2 tog *(Fig. 14, page 46)*, P1, leave remaining 8 sts unworked; turn.

Row 3: Slip 1, K {6-8-10}{12-14-16}, SSK, K1; turn.

Row 4: Slip 1, P {7-9-11}{13-15-17}, P2 tog, P1; turn.

Rows 5-10: Repeat Rows 3 and 4, 3 times adding one st before decrease: {16-18-20}{22-24-26} sts.

GUSSET

The remainder of the sock will be worked in rounds.

Slip the Instep sts from the st holders onto 2 double pointed needles, {13-14-15}{16-17-18} sts each.

FOUNDATION ROUND

With **right** side of Heel facing, using an empty double pointed needle and continuing with the working yarn, knit {8-9-10}{11-12-13} of the Heel sts.
Place a split-ring marker around the next st to indicate the beginning of the round *(see Markers, page 43)*. Using an empty double pointed needle (this will be needle 1), knit across the remaining {8-9-10}{11-12-13} Heel sts. With the same needle, pick up {13-14-15}{16-17-18} sts along the side of the Heel Flap *(Fig. 16a, page 46)* and one st in the corner. With separate needles, knit across the Instep sts (needles 2 and 3).

With an empty needle, pick up one st in the corner and {13-14-15}{16-17-18} sts along the side of the Heel Flap. With the same needle, knit {8-9-10}{11-12-13} Heel sts.

Stitch count is {22-24-26}{28-30-32} sts on the first needle, {13-14-15}{16-17-18} sts each on the second and third needles, and {22-24-26}{28-30-32} sts on fourth needle for a total of {70-76-82}{88-94-100} sts.

GUSSET DECREASES
Rnd 1 (Decrease rnd): Knit across to the last 3 sts on first needle, K2 tog *(Fig. 10, page 45)*, K1; knit across the second and third needles; on fourth needle, K1, SSK, knit across: {68-74-80}{86-92-98} sts.

Rnd 2: Knit around.

Rnds 3 thru {18-20-22}{24-26-28}: Repeat Rnds 1 and 2, {8-9-10}{11-12-13} times: {52-56-60}{64-68-72} sts, {13-14-15}{16-17-18} sts on each needle.

FOOT
Work even knitting each round until Foot measures approximately {7$\frac{1}{4}$-7$\frac{1}{2}$-8}{8$\frac{1}{2}$-8$\frac{3}{4}$-9}"/ {18.5-19-20.5}{21.5-22-23} cm from back of Heel **or** {1$\frac{1}{2}$-1$\frac{3}{4}$-2}{1$\frac{3}{4}$-2-2$\frac{1}{4}$}"/{4-4.5-5}{4.5-5-5.5} cm less than total desired Foot length from back of Heel to Toe.

TOE
Rnd 1 (Decrease rnd): Knit across first needle to last 3 sts, K2 tog, K1; on second needle, K1, SSK, knit across; on third needle, knit across to last 3 sts, K2 tog, K1; on fourth needle, K1, SSK, knit across: 4 sts decreased.

Rnd 2: Knit around.

Repeat Rnds 1 and 2, {6-7-8}{7-8-9} times: {6-6-6}{8-8-8} sts on each needle.

Using the fourth needle, knit across the sts on the first needle; cut yarn leaving a long end.

Slip the stitches from the third needle onto the second needle, so there are the same amount on the first and second needles.

GRAFTING
Thread the yarn needle with the long end. Hold the threaded yarn needle on the right-hand side of work.
Work in the following sequence, pulling yarn through as if to knit or as if to purl with even tension and keeping yarn under points of needles to avoid tangling and extra loops.
Step 1: Purl first stitch on **front** needle, leave on *(Fig. 3a)*.
Step 2: Knit first stitch on **back** needle, leave on *(Fig. 3b)*.
Step 3: Knit first stitch on **front** needle, slip off.
Step 4: Purl next stitch on **front** needle, leave on.
Step 5: Purl first stitch on **back** needle, slip off.
Step 6: Knit next stitch on **back** needle, leave on.
Repeat Steps 3-6 across until all stitches are worked off the needles.

Fig. 3a

Fig. 3b

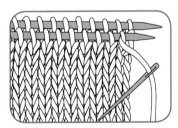
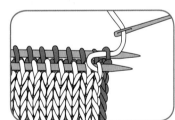

Repeat for second Sock.

Lydia's Tip: Socks can be blocked by placing them under a damp towel.

afghan to crochet

Lydia's sister Margaret is usually a glass-half-empty kind of woman. But where crochet is concerned, Margaret is all enthusiasm. This popcorn-patterned afghan is similar to the one she was speedily creating at the baseball game.

■■■□ INTERMEDIATE

Finished Size: 46" x 65" (117 cm x 165 cm)

MATERIALS
Medium Weight Yarn 🔲**4**
[3.5 ounces, 241 yards
(100 grams, 220 meters) per skein]:
  Brown - 8 skeins
  Blue - 4 skeins
Crochet hook, size H (5 mm) **or** size needed
  for gauge

GAUGE: In pattern,
    2 repeats = 11½" (29.25 cm)
    5 rows = 4" (10 cm)

Gauge Swatch: 11½" x 4" (29.25 cm x 10 cm)
Ch 53.
Rows 1-5: Work same as Body.
Finish off.

STITCH GUIDE

DOUBLE DECREASE (uses next 3 sts)
★ YO, insert hook in **next** st, YO and pull up a loop, YO and draw through 2 loops on hook; repeat from ★ 2 times **more**, YO and draw through all 4 loops on hook (**counts as one dc).**

CENTER DECREASE (uses next 5 sts)
★ YO, insert hook in **next** st, YO and pull up a loop, YO and draw through 2 loops on hook; repeat from ★ 4 times **more**, YO and draw through all 6 loops on hook (**counts as one dc).**
POPCORN (uses one st)
5 Dc in dc indicated, drop loop from hook, insert hook in first dc of 5-dc group, hook dropped loop and draw through st to form Popcorn *(Fig. 18, page 47).*

CHANGING COLORS
Change color as you are working the last dc in the row as follows: YO, insert hook in last dc, YO and pull up a loop, YO and draw through 2 loops on hook, cut yarn; with new yarn, YO and draw through both loops on hook *(Fig. 19, page 47).*

BODY
With Brown, chain 197.

Row 1 (Right side)**:** Skipping first 3 chs from hook, work double decrease (**3 skipped chs count as first dc**), dc in next 9 chs, 5 dc in next ch, dc in next 9 chs, ★ work center decrease, dc in next 9 chs, 5 dc in next ch, dc in next 9 chs; repeat from ★ across to last 4 chs, work double decrease, dc in last ch: 195 dc.

Row 2: Ch 3 (**counts as first dc, now and throughout**), turn; work double decrease, dc in next 9 dc, 5 dc in next dc, dc in next 9 dc, ★ work center decrease, dc in next 9 dc, 5 dc in next dc, dc in next 9 dc; repeat from ★ across to last 4 dc, work double decrease, dc in last dc.

Instructions continued on page 38.

At Stitch and
Pitch night at the
Mariners game,
Margaret scooted
past several others
in order to sit next
to Lydia. Knitters sat
on every side and the
mood was jovial as
they displayed their
current efforts to one
another. Margaret's
fingers moved the
crochet hook with
amazing speed and
dexterity. She looked
to be working on
an afghan.

—Summer on
Blossom Street

Row 3: Ch 3, turn; work double decrease, ★ † ch 1, (skip next dc, dc in next dc, ch 1) 4 times, skip next dc, 5 dc in next dc, ch 1, (skip next dc, dc in next dc, ch 1) 4 times, skip next dc †, work center decrease; repeat from ★ 6 times **more**, then repeat from † to † once, work double decrease, dc in last dc changing to Blue: 115 dc and 80 ch-1 sps.

Row 4: Ch 3, turn; work double decrease, ★ † dc in next ch-1 sp, (dc in next dc and in next ch-1 sp) 3 times, dc in next 2 dc, 5 dc in next dc, dc in next 2 dc and in next ch-1 sp, (dc in next dc and in next ch-1 sp) 3 times †, work center decrease; repeat from ★ 6 times **more**, then repeat from † to † once, work double decrease, dc in last dc: 195 dc.

Row 5: Ch 3, turn; work double decrease, ★ † ch 1, (skip next dc, work Popcorn in next dc, ch 1) 4 times, skip next dc, work (Popcorn, ch 2, Popcorn) in next dc, ch 1, (skip next dc, work Popcorn in next dc, ch 1) 4 times, skip next dc †, work center decrease; repeat from ★ 6 times **more**, then repeat from † to † once, work double decrease, dc in last dc: 80 Popcorns and 88 sps.

Row 6: Ch 3, turn; work double decrease, ★ † (dc in next ch-1 sp and in next Popcorn) 4 times, 7 dc in next ch-2 sp, (dc in next Popcorn and in next ch-1 sp) 4 times †, work center decrease; repeat from ★ 6 times **more**, then repeat from † to † once, work double decrease, dc in last dc changing to Brown: 195 dc.

Row 7: Ch 3, turn; work double decrease, ★ † ch 1, (skip next dc, dc in next dc, ch 1) 4 times, skip next dc, 5 dc in next dc, ch 1, (skip next dc, dc in next dc, ch 1) 4 times, skip next dc †, work center decrease; repeat from ★ 6 times **more**, then repeat from † to † once, work double decrease, dc in last dc: 115 dc and 80 ch-1 sps.

Rows 8 and 9: Repeat Rows 4 and 5.

Row 10: Ch 3, turn; work double decrease, ★ † (dc in next ch-1 sp and in next Popcorn) 4 times, 7 dc in next ch-2 sp, (dc in next Popcorn and in next ch-1 sp) 4 times †, work center decrease; repeat from ★ 6 times **more**, then repeat from † to † once, work double decrease, dc in last dc: 195 dc.

Rows 11-16: Repeat Rows 3-8.

Rows 17-22: Ch 3, turn; work double decrease, dc in next 9 dc, 5 dc in next dc, dc in next 9 dc, ★ work center decrease, dc in next 9 dc, 5 dc in next dc, dc in next 9 dc; repeat from ★ across to last 4 dc, work double decrease, dc in last dc.

Rows 23-77: Repeat Rows 3-22 twice, then repeat Rows 3-17 once **more**.

Finish off.

Row 18: P1, K1, (K2 tog, YO) 3 times, ★ (P1, K1) 3 times, (K2 tog, YO) 3 times; repeat from ★ across to last 8 sts, (P1, K1) across.

Row 19: K1, (P1, K1) 3 times, P7, ★ K1, (P1, K1) twice, P7; repeat from ★ across to last 2 sts, K1, P1.

Rows 20-27: Repeat Rows 16-19 twice.

Rows 28 thru 207{231-279}: Repeat Rows 4-27, 7{8-10} times; then repeat Rows 4-15 once **more**.

Bind off all sts in **knit**.

FINISHING

With **right** sides together, using diagram as a guide for placement, and matching blocks to continue checkerboard pattern, sew bound off edge of second Panel to left side of first Panel. Sew bound off edge of first Panel to edge of second Panel.

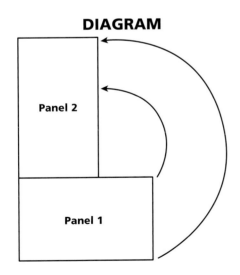

DIAGRAM

Panel 2

Panel 1

FINISHING
ASSEMBLY
Arrange Squares in desired order. Working through inside loops only, whipstitch Squares together **(Fig. 22, page 48)**, forming 5 vertical stripes of 7 Squares each, beginning in first corner and ending in next corner; then whipstitch strips together in same manner.

EDGING
Rnd 1: With **right** side facing, join either color with slip st in any corner sp; ch 1, (sc, ch 3) twice in same sp, ★ (sc in next ch-1 sp, ch 3) 6 times, † sc in joining, ch 3, (sc in next ch-1 sp, ch 3) 6 times †, repeat from † to † across to next corner sp, (sc, ch 3) twice in corner sp; repeat from ★ 2 times **more**, (sc in next ch-1 sp, ch 3) 6 times, repeat from † to † across; join with slip st to first sc: 172 sc and 172 ch-3 sps.

Rnd 2: Slip st in first corner sp, ch 3, (2 dc, ch 1, 3 dc) in same sp, ch 1, ★ (3 dc in next ch-3 sp, ch 1) across to next corner ch-3 sp, (3 dc, ch 1) twice in corner ch-3 sp; repeat from ★ 2 times **more**, (3 dc in next ch-3 sp, ch 1) across; join with slip st to first dc, finish off.

Design by Cathy Hardy.

thank you for helping warm up america!

Since 1991, Warm Up America! has donated more than 250,000 afghans to battered women's shelters, victims of natural disaster, the homeless, and many others who are in need.

You can help Warm Up America! help others, and with so little effort. Debbie urges everyone who uses the patterns in this book to take a few minutes to work a 7" x 9" block for this worthy cause. To help you get started, she's providing these two block patterns, one to knit and one to crochet.

If you are able to provide a completed afghan, Warm Up America! requests that you donate it directly to any charity or social services agency in your community. If you require assistance in assembling the blocks into an afghan, please include your name and address inside the packaging and ship your 7" x 9" blocks to:

> Warm Up America! Foundation
> 2500 Lowell Road
> Ranlo, NC 28054

Remember, just a little bit of yarn can make a big difference to someone in need!

Basic patchwork afghans are made of forty-nine 7" x 9" (18 cm x 23 cm) rectangular blocks that are sewn together. Any pattern stitch can be used for the rectangle. Use acrylic medium weight yarn. For a knit block use size 8 (5 mm) straight knitting needles or size needed to obtain the gauge of 9 stitches to 2" (5 cm). For a crochet block use size H (5 mm) crochet hook or size needed to obtain the gauge of 8 double crochets to 2" (5 cm).

Knit Block

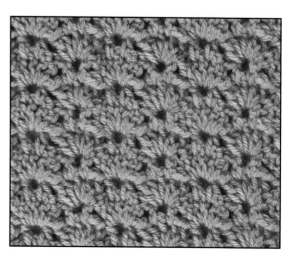

Crochet Block

KNIT QUILTED LACE BLOCK

Multiple of 6 sts + 1.

When instructed to slip stitches, always slip as if to **purl**, with yarn held **loosely** in **front**.

Cast on 31 sts.

Row 1 AND ALL WRONG SIDE ROWS: Purl across.

Row 2: K4, slip 5, (K1, slip 5) 3 times, K4.

Row 4: K6, K1 under strand *(Fig. 4)*, (K5, K1 under strand) 3 times, K6.

Fig. 4

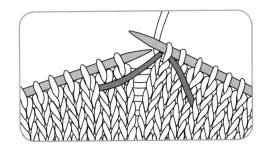

Row 6: K3, slip 3, K1, (slip 5, K1) 3 times, slip 3, K3.

Row 8: K3, K1 under strand, (K5, K1 under strand) 4 times, K3.

Repeat Rows 1-8 for pattern until Block measures approximately 9" (23 cm) from cast on edge, ending by working Row 1 or Row 5.

Bind off all sts in **knit**.

ASSEMBLY

Sew Blocks together, forming 7 vertical strips of 7 Blocks each and measuring 7" x 63" (18 cm x 160 cm); sew strips together in same manner.

Weave in all yarn ends.

CROCHET SWEET PEA BLOCK

Multiple of 7 sts.

Ch 28.

Row 1 (Right side): Dc in fourth ch from hook **(3 skipped chs count as first dc)**, ★ skip next 2 chs, 5 dc in next ch (5-dc group), skip next 2 chs, dc in next 2 chs (2-dc group); repeat from ★ across to last 3 chs, skip next 2 chs, 3 dc in last ch: 3 5-dc groups.

Note: Loop a short piece of yarn around any stitch to mark Row 1 as **right** side.

Row 2: Ch 3 **(counts as first dc, now and throughout)**, turn; dc in sp **before** next dc *(Fig. 21, page 47)*, ★ 5 dc in sp **between** dc of next 2-dc group, dc in sp **between** second and third dc of next 5-dc group and in next sp (between third and fourth dc); repeat from ★ across to last 4 dc, skip next 3 dc, 3 dc in sp before last dc.

Repeat Row 2 for pattern until Block measures approximately 8½" (21.5 cm) from beginning ch; do **not** finish off.

Edging: Ch 1, with **right** side facing, work sc evenly spaced around working 3 sc in each corner; join with slip st to first sc, finish off.

Assemble same as for Knit Blocks.

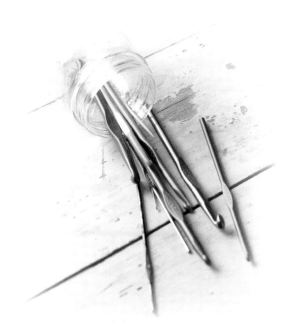

general instructions

ABBREVIATIONS

C4B	cable 4 back
C6B	cable 6 back
C4F	cable 4 front
C6F	cable 6 front
ch	chain
cm	centimeters
dc	double crochet(s)
K	knit
mm	millimeters
P	purl
P2SSO	pass 2 slipped stitches over
Rnd(s)	round(s)
sc	single crochet(s)
sp(s)	space(s)
SSK	slip, slip, knit
SSP	slip, slip, purl
st(s)	stitch(es)
tbl	through back loop
tog	together
YO	yarn over

★ — work instructions following ★ as many **more** times as indicated in addition to the first time.

† to † — work all instructions from first † to second † **as many** times as specified.

( ) or [ ] — work enclosed instructions **as many** times as specified by the number immediately following **or** work all enclosed instructions in the stitch or space indicated **or** contains explanatory remarks.

colon (:) — the number given after a colon at the end of a row or round denotes the number of stitches or spaces you should have on that row or round.

work even — work without increasing or decreasing in the established pattern.

KNIT TERMINOLOGY

UNITED STATES		INTERNATIONAL
gauge	=	tension
bind off	=	cast off
yarn over (YO)	=	yarn forward (yfwd) **or** yarn around needle (yrn)

Yarn Weight Symbol & Names	LACE 0	SUPER FINE 1	FINE 2	LIGHT 3	MEDIUM 4	BULKY 5	SUPER BULKY 6
Type of Yarns in Category	Fingering, size 10 crochet thread	Sock, Fingering, Baby	Sport, Baby	DK, Light Worsted	Worsted, Afghan, Aran	Chunky, Craft, Rug	Bulky, Roving
Knit Gauge Range* in Stockinette St to 4" (10 cm)	33-40** sts	27-32 sts	23-26 sts	21-24 sts	16-20 sts	12-15 sts	6-11 sts
Advised Needle Size Range	000-1	1 to 3	3 to 5	5 to 7	7 to 9	9 to 11	11 and larger

*GUIDELINES ONLY: The chart above reflects the most commonly used gauges and needle sizes for specific yarn categories.

** Lace weight yarns are usually knitted on larger needles to create lacy openwork patterns. Accordingly, a gauge range is difficult to determine. Always follow the gauge stated in your pattern.

KNITTING NEEDLES

U.S.	0	1	2	3	4	5	6	7	8	9	10	10½	11	13	15	17
U.K.	13	12	11	10	9	8	7	6	5	4	3	2	1	00	000	---
Metric - mm	2	2.25	2.75	3.25	3.5	3.75	4	4.5	5	5.5	6	6.5	8	9	10	12.75

■□□□ BEGINNER	Projects for first-time knitters using basic knit and purl stitches. Minimal shaping.
■■□□ EASY	Projects using basic stitches, repetitive stitch patterns, simple color changes, and simple shaping and finishing.
■■■□ INTERMEDIATE	Projects with a variety of stitches, such as basic cables and lace, simple intarsia, double-pointed needles and knitting in the round needle techniques, mid-level shaping and finishing.
■■■■ EXPERIENCED	Projects using advanced techniques and stitches, such as short rows, fair isle, more intricate intarsia, cables, lace patterns, and numerous color changes.

GAUGE

Exact gauge is **essential** for proper size. Before beginning your project, make a sample swatch in the yarn and needle or hook specified in the individual instructions. After completing the swatch, measure it, counting your stitches and rows or rounds carefully. If your swatch is larger or smaller than specified, **make another, changing needle or hook size to get the correct gauge.** Keep trying until you find the size needles or hook that will give you the specified gauge. Once proper gauge is obtained, measure width of project approximately every 3" (7.5 cm) to be sure gauge remains consistent.

MARKERS

As a convenience to you, we have used markers to mark the beginning of a round, help distinguish the beginning of a pattern, or to mark placement of decreases. Place markers as instructed. You may use purchased markers or tie a length of contrasting color yarn around the needle. When you reach a marker on each row or round, slip it from the left needle to the right needle; remove it when no longer needed.

ZEROS

To consolidate the length of an involved pattern, zeros are sometimes used so that all sizes can be combined. For example, increase every fourth row {0-11-7} times means that the first size would do nothing, the second size would increase 11 times, and the largest size would increase 7 times.

●□□□ BEGINNER	Projects for first-time crocheters using basic stitches. Minimal shaping.
●■□□ EASY	Projects using yarn with basic stitches, repetitive stitch patterns, simple color changes, and simple shaping and finishing.
●■■□ INTERMEDIATE	Projects using a variety of techniques, such as basic lace patterns or color patterns, mid-level shaping and finishing.
●■■■ EXPERIENCED	Projects with intricate stitch patterns, techniques and dimension, such as non-repeating patterns, multi-color techniques, fine threads, small hooks, detailed shaping and refined finishing.

CROCHET HOOKS

U.S.	B-1	C-2	D-3	E-4	F-5	G-6	H-8	I-9	J-10	K-10½	N	P	Q
Metric - mm	2.25	2.75	3.25	3.5	3.75	4	5	5.5	6	6.5	9	10	15

Yarn Weight Symbol & Names	LACE 0	SUPER FINE 1	FINE 2	LIGHT 3	MEDIUM 4	BULKY 5	SUPER BULKY 6
Type of Yarns in Category	Fingering, 10-count crochet thread	Sock, Fingering Baby	Sport, Baby	DK, Light Worsted	Worsted, Afghan, Aran	Chunky, Craft, Rug	Bulky, Roving
Crochet Gauge* Ranges in Single Crochet to 4" (10 cm)	32-42 double crochets**	21-32 sts	16-20 sts	12-17 sts	11-14 sts	8-11 sts	5-9 sts
Advised Hook Size Range	Steel*** 6,7,8 Regular hook B-1	B-1 to E-4	E-4 to 7	7 to I-9	I-9 to K-10.5	K-10.5 to M-13	M-13 and larger

CROCHET TERMINOLOGY	
UNITED STATES	INTERNATIONAL
slip stitch (slip st) =	single crochet (sc)
single crochet (sc) =	double crochet (dc)
half double crochet (hdc) =	half treble crochet (htr)
double crochet (dc) =	treble crochet(tr)
treble crochet (tr) =	double treble crochet (dtr)
double treble crochet (dtr) =	triple treble crochet (ttr)
triple treble crochet (tr tr) =	quadruple treble crochet (qtr)
skip =	miss

*GUIDELINES ONLY: The chart above reflects the most commonly used gauges and hook sizes for specific yarn categories.

** Lace weight yarns are usually crocheted on larger-size hooks to create lacy openwork patterns. Accordingly, a gauge range is difficult to determine. Always follow the gauge stated in your pattern.

*** Steel crochet hooks are sized differently from regular hooks—the higher the number the smaller the hook, which is the reverse of regular hook sizing.

DOUBLE POINTED NEEDLES

The stitches are divided evenly between four double pointed needles as specified in the individual pattern. Form a square with the four needles. Do **not** twist the cast on ridge. With the remaining needle, work across the stitches on the first needle *(Fig. 5)*. You will now have an empty needle with which to work the stitches from the next needle. Work the first stitch of each needle firmly to prevent gaps. Continue working around without turning the work.

Fig. 5

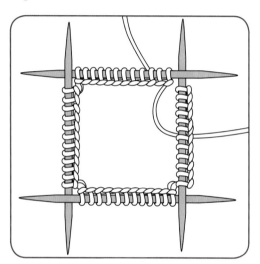

THROUGH BACK LOOP
(abbreviated tbl)

When instructed to knit or purl into the back loop of a stitch *(Fig. 6)*, the result will be twisted stitches.

Fig. 6

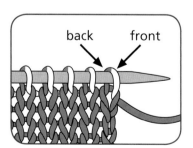

YARN OVERS

After a knit stitch, before a knit stitch
Bring the yarn forward **between** the needles, then back **over** the top of the right hand needle, so that it is now in position to knit the next stitch *(Fig. 7a)*.

Fig. 7a

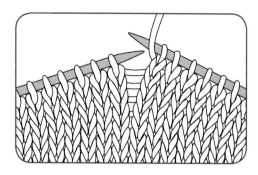

After a knit stitch, before a purl stitch
Bring the yarn forward **between** the needles, then back **over** the top of the right hand needle and forward **between** the needles again, so that it is now in position to purl the next stitch *(Fig. 7b)*.

Fig. 7b

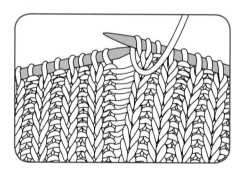

KNIT INCREASE

Knit the next stitch but do **not** slip the old stitch off the left needle *(Fig. 8a)*. Insert the right needle into the **back** loop of the **same** stitch and knit it *(Fig. 8b)*, then slip the old stitch off the left needle.

Fig. 8a

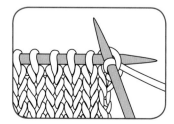

Fig. 8b

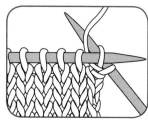

INVISIBLE INCREASE

Insert the right needle from the **front** into the side of the stitch **below** the next stitch on the left needle **(Fig. 9)** and knit it, then knit the next stitch.

Fig. 9

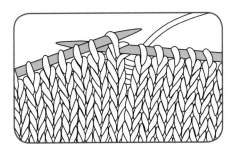

DECREASES

KNIT 2 TOGETHER (abbreviated K2 tog)

Insert the right needle into the **front** of the first two stitches on the left needle as if to **knit** **(Fig. 10)**, then **knit** them together as if they were one stitch.

Fig. 10

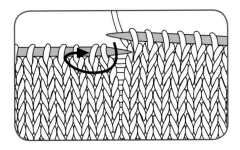

KNIT 2 TOGETHER THROUGH BACK LOOP (abbreviated K2 tog tbl)

Insert the right needle into the **back** of the first two stitches on the left needle **(Fig. 11)**, then **knit** them together as if they were one stitch.

Fig. 11

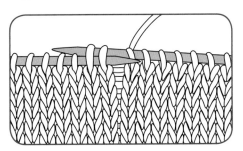

SLIP, SLIP, KNIT (abbreviated SSK)

Slip the first stitch as if to **knit**, then slip the next stitch as if to **knit** **(Fig. 12a)**. Insert the **left** needle into the **front** of both slipped stitches **(Fig. 12b)** and knit them together as if they were one stitch **(Fig. 12c)**.

Fig. 12a

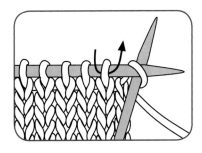

Fig. 12b

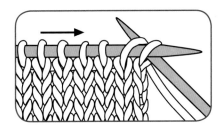

Fig. 12c

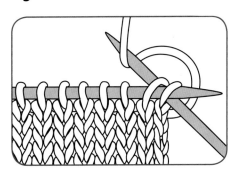

SLIP 2, KNIT 1, PASS 2 SLIPPED STITCHES OVER
(abbreviated slip 2, K1, P2SSO)
Slip two stitches separately as if to **knit** *(Fig. 12a, page 45)*, then knit the next stitch. With the left needle, bring the two slipped stitches over the stitch just made and off the needle *(Fig. 13)*.

Fig. 13

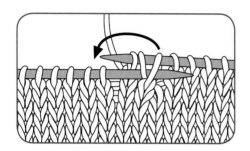

PURL 2 TOGETHER *(abbreviated P2 tog)*
Insert the right needle into the **front** of the first two stitches on the left needle as if to **purl** *(Fig. 14)*, then **purl** them together as if they were one stitch.

Fig. 14

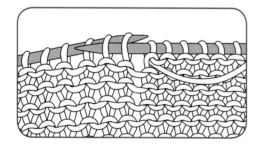

SLIP, SLIP, PURL *(abbreviated SSP)*
Slip the first stitch as if to **knit**, then slip the next stitch as if to **knit** *(Fig. 12a, page 45)*. Place these two stitches back onto the left needle. Insert the **right** needle into the **back** of both slipped stitches from the **back** to **front** *(Fig. 15)* and purl them together as if they were one stitch.

Fig. 15

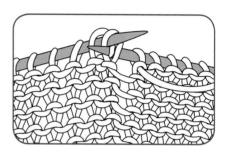

PICKING UP STITCHES
When instructed to pick up stitches, insert the needle from the **front** to the **back** under two strands at the edge of the worked piece *(Fig. 16a or b)*. Put the yarn around the needle as if to **knit**, then bring the needle with the yarn back through the stitch to the right side, resulting in a stitch on the needle.
Repeat this along the edge, picking up the required number of stitches.
A crochet hook may be helpful to pull yarn through.

Fig. 16a

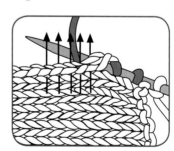

Fig. 16b

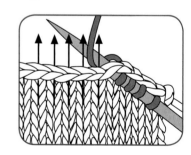

WEAVING SEAMS

With the **right** side of both pieces facing you and edges even, sew through both pieces once to secure the beginning of the seam, leaving an ample yarn end to weave in later. Insert the needle under the bar **between** the first and second stitches on the row and pull the yarn through *(Fig. 17)*. Insert the needle under the next bar on the second side. Repeat from side to side, being careful to match rows. If the edges are different lengths, it may be necessary to insert the needle under two bars at one edge.

Fig. 17

CROCHET STITCHES
POPCORN *(uses one st)*

Work 5 dc in st indicated, drop loop from hook, insert hook in first dc of 5-dc group, hook dropped loop and draw through stitch *(Fig. 18)*.

Fig. 18

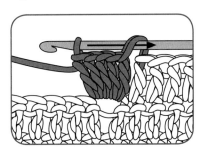

CHANGING COLORS

YO, insert hook in stitch indicated, YO and pull up a loop, YO and draw through 2 loops on hook, cut yarn, with new yarn *(Fig. 19)*, YO and draw through 2 loops on hook.

Fig. 19

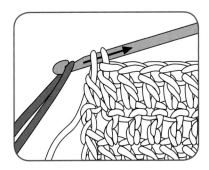

BACK & FRONT LOOPS ONLY

Work only in loop(s) indicated by arrow *(Fig. 20)*.

Fig. 20

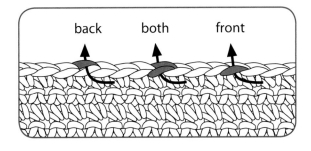

WORKING IN SPACE BEFORE A STITCH

When instructed to work in space before a stitch or in spaces between stitches, insert hook in space indicated by arrow *(Fig. 21)*.

Fig. 21

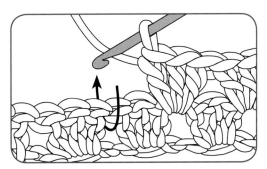

WHIPSTITCH

Place two Squares with **wrong** sides together. Beginning in corner ch, sew through **both** pieces once to secure the beginning of the seam, leaving an ample yarn end to weave in later. Insert the needle from **front** to **back** through **inside** loops only of each stitch on both pieces *(Fig. 22)*. Bring the needle around and insert it from **front** to **back** through next loops of both pieces. Continue in this manner across to corner, keeping the sewing yarn fairly loose.

Fig. 22

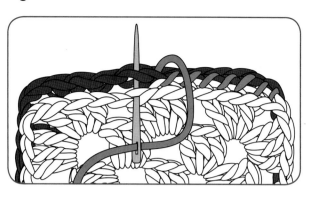

yarn information

The projects in this leaflet were made using a variety of yarns. Any brand in the specified weight may be used. It is best to refer to the yardage/meters when determining how many balls or skeins to purchase. Remember, to arrive at the finished size, it is the GAUGE/TENSION that is important, not the brand of yarn. For your convenience, listed below are the specific yarns used to create our photography models.

CABLE SAMPLER SCARF
Fiber Trends Inc.
Naturally Yarns Harmony
#700 Aran

BABY BLANKET
Bernat® Softee® Baby
#31744 Funny Prints

WASHCLOTH TO CROCHET
Bernat® Handicrafter® Cotton
#23741 Playtime
#23743 Summer Splash
#23744 Swimming Pool

MEMORIES OF PARIS SCARF
Anny Blatt Angora Super
#494 Ruban

PONCHO
Caron® Country
#0013 Spruce

CODY'S PULLOVER
Lion Brand® Vanna's Choice®
#174 Olive
Lion Brand® Vanna's Choice® Baby
#128 Chocolate Cake

REESE'S VEST
Knit Picks® Andean Treasure Yarn
#23488 Granite Heather

LAP ROBE TO CROCHET
Lion Brand® Cotton-Ease®
#103 Blossom
#145 Plum

SOCKS FOR HUTCH
Patons® Kroy Socks
#55613 Cyan Stripes

AFGHAN TO CROCHET
Patons® Canadiana
#00130 Light Wedgewood
#10012 Dark Beige

WARM UP AMERICA
Lion Brand® Vanna's Choice®
#172 Kelly Green
Lion Brand® Vanna's Choice® Baby
#106 Little Boy Blue

Instructions tested and photo models made by Janet Akins, JoAnn Bowling, Lee Ellis, Sue Galucki, Raymelle Greening, Dale Potter, and Ted Tomany.